ROBERT LOUIS STEVENSON'S

TREASURE ISLAND

by Robert Louis Stevenson
retold by Wim Coleman and Pat Perrin
illustrated by Greg Rebis

Librarian Reviewer
Allyson A.W. Lyga MS
Library Media/Graphic Novel Consultant
Fulbright Memorial Fund Scholar, author

Reading Consultant
Mark DeYoung
Classroom Teacher, Edina Public Schools, MN
BA in Elementary Education, Central College
MS in Curriculum & Instruction, University of Minnesota

Graphic Revolve is published by Stone Arch Books,
151 Good Counsel Drive, P.O. Box 669,
Mankato, Minnesota 56002.
www.stonearchbooks.com

Library of Congress Cataloging-in-Publication Data
Coleman, Wim.
  Treasure Island / by Robert Louis Stevenson; retold by Wim Coleman and Pat
Perrin; illustrated by Greg Rebis.
  p. cm.—(Graphic Revolve)
  ISBN-13: 978-1-59889-050-1 (hardcover)
  ISBN-10: 1-59889-050-6 (hardcover)
  ISBN-13: 978-1-59889-222-2 (paperback)
  ISBN-10: 1-59889-222-3 (paperback)
  1. Graphic novels. I. Perrin, Pat. II. Rebis, Greg. III. Stevenson, Robert Louis,
1850–1894. Treasure Island. IV. Title. V. Series.
PN6727.C5725T74 2007
741.5'973—dc22   2006007695

Summary: Young Jim Hawkins discovers an old treasure map and sets out on a
harrowing voyage to a faraway island. The violent sea is just the first of many
obstacles, as Jim soon learns there are dangerous men seeking the same treasure.

Credits
Art Director: Heather Kindseth
Graphic Designers: Heather Kindseth and Kay Fraser
Colorists: Greg Rebis, Dylan Edwards, Tiffany Moore,
Leila Hill, Melissa Armstrong and Katherine Rebis

1 2 3 4 5 6 11 10 09 08 07 06

Printed in the United States of America.

TABLE OF CONTENTS

Jim Hawkins

Ben Gunn

Billy Bones

Dr. Livesey

4

Mr. Trelawney

Captain Smollett

Long John Silver

Israel Hands

13

25

27

Ben Gunn quickly shares his story. He had been part of Captain Flint's crew, along with Long John Silver and Billy Bones, when Flint buried his treasure on the island.

By the time the fighting ends, only eight pirates are left alive. Five of the crew remain, but the captain is badly hurt.

The next day, while the men are tending their wounds and burying the dead, Jim grabs a couple of guns and sneaks away.

He finds Ben Gunn's boat.

I'll row out to the ship as soon as it's dark.

Two sailors argue aboard the ship.

I ought to kill you, you dog!.

Then the *Hispaniola* comes into view.

If I can get aboard her . . .

46

Just then the ship crashes into the shore.

CREEEEEEEAK KRUNCH

I have to reload. I haven't a second to lose!

I've done it! I've taken back the ship!

You've messed up everything, John Silver.

We don't have a ship or the treasure now.

Ah, but we do have a prisoner.

And we have this map. Dr. Livesey gave it to me as part of our deal.

Remember this, Jim. I just saved your life.

The next morning, Jim is surprised to see Dr. Livesey tending to the pirates' wounds.

I've done my duty. Now let me speak to Jim.

Quickly, Jim tells Dr. Livesey where the ship is.

All right, but the boy has promised that he won't try to escape.

Inside Ben Gunn's cave . . .

It'll take us a few days to get all this aboard the *Hispaniola*.

After they load the treasure onto the ship, Captain Smollett, Dr. Livesey, Mr. Trelawney, Long John Silver, and Jim Hawkins sail away from Treasure Island.

Don't leave us!

We needn't waste our pity on those dogs!

For once I agree with you, Silver.

The *Hispaniola* sails to a port in Mexico, where Captain Smollett hires some new crew members.

While the ship is in port, Long John escapes.

I did it! I helped him escape. If Silver had stayed aboard, we'd have ended up dead.

About Robert Louis Stevenson

Robert Louis Stevenson was born in 1850 in Edinburgh, Scotland. He enjoyed traveling and having adventures. During one family vacation in Scotland, Stevenson and his stepson amused themselves by drawing a treasure map for an imaginary island. The stories he and his stepson told inspired Stevenson to write *Treasure Island.* It was published in 1883. Stevenson's other famous books include *Kidnapped* and *The Strange Case of Dr. Jekyll and Mr. Hyde.* He died in 1894.

About the Retelling Authors

Wim Coleman and Pat Perrin are a married couple who love writing books together. They have written many young adult nonfiction and fiction books, including retellings of classic novels, stories, and myths. They run a scholarship program for Mexican students and live in Guanajuato, Mexico.

About the Illustrator

Greg Rebis was born in Queens, New York, but grew up mostly in central Florida. After working in civic government, pizza delivery, music retail and proofreading, he eventually landed work in publishing, film and graphics. He currently lives and studies in Rhode Island and still loves art, sci-fi and video games.

GLOSSARY

ashore (uh-SHOR) — on or toward the shore or land

beach (BEECH) — to land a ship on the shore

curiosity (kyur-ee-AHSS-i-tee) — wanting to know more about things

Hispaniola (HISS-span-ee-oh-la) — Captain Smollett's ship

inn (IN) — a small hotel, often with a restaurant

magistrate (MAJ-uh-strate) — a government official or judge who has the power to enforce the law

mate (MAYT) — a friend or person that someone works with

pieces of eight (PEESS-iz uhv ATE) — in pirate times, the Spanish currency was the peso, which was worth eight reales. Sometimes, a pirate would break the peso coin into eight pieces to make change.

request (re-KWEST) — something that is asked for

seaman (SEE-man) — a sailor

shipwrecked (SHIP-rekd) — a ship that has been destroyed at sea

tending to (TEN-ding TOO) — taking care of

truce (TROOS) — an agreement to stop fighting

Background of Treasure Island

In the 1700s, the world of Jim Hawkins was full of sailing ships. People crossed the oceans, transported goods, and explored new lands using wind power and strong ocean currents. In seaside towns, ships were loaded along the wharves, or docks. A captain called his ship "shipshape" or "seaworthy" if it was ready to go to sea. And when the captain yelled "all hands on deck," the crew boarded, ready to work.

Each person on a ship had their own special job to do. Cabin boys, hoping to learn more about sailing, served the captain. The captain steered the ship by turning the ship's tiller. Crew members would lift and lower the heavy sails. To keep the ship in one place, the crew would drop an anchor, or heavy weight. If a ship went adrift, meaning that it floated off course, the crew sometimes stopped it by sailing it onto land, or beaching it. The life of a sailor was hard, and not all crew members made it home alive.

Ships traveled on the "high seas," waters that were not owned by any country. Life at sea was full of danger. A ship could sink in a storm or become shipwrecked. Crews could be stranded on strange islands or coastlines. Pirates could attack. To show they were in command of a ship, pirates would "raise the Jolly Roger," hang a black flag with a skull and crossbones from a high mast.

Discussion Questions

1. Why did Billy Bones die?

2. How did Jim figure out that Long John Silver was the one-legged pirate that Billy Bones told him about?

3. What would you do if you found a buried treasure?

4. Why did Jim sneak onto one of the small boats when the pirates went to look for buried treasure?

WRITING PROMPTS

1. At the end of the story, the pirates flee and the remaining crew members of the *Hispaniola* divide the treasure. How did each person spend the treasure? What does this tell you about each person?

2. Describe your favorite character in *Treasure Island*. Why do you like this character? Would you want to sail on a ship with this person?

3. If you could pick any place in the world to have an adventure, where would you go? Explain how you would get there and what you would discover.

Other Books

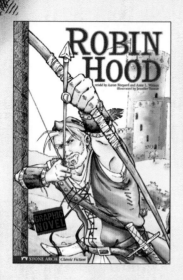

Robin Hood

Robin Hood and his Merrie Men are the heroes of Sherwood Forest. Taking from the rich and giving to the poor, Robin Hood and his loyal followers fight for the downtrodden and oppressed. As they outwit the cruel Sheriff of Nottingham, Robin Hood and his Merrie Men are led on a series of exciting adventures.

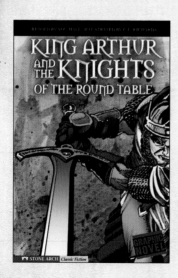

King Arthur and the Knights of the Round Table

In a world of wizards, giants, and dragons, King Arthur and the Knights of the Round Table are the kingdom of Camelot's only defense against the threatening forces of evil. Fighting battles and saving those in need, the Knights of the Round Table can defeat every enemy but one – themselves!

The Hunchback of Notre Dame

Hidden away in the bell tower of the Cathedral of Notre Dame, Quasimodo is treated like a beast. Although he is gentle and kind, he has the reputation of a frightening monster because of his physical deformities. He develops affection for Esmeralda, a gypsy girl who shows him kindness in return. When the girl is sentenced to an unfair death by hanging, Quasimodo is determined to save her. But those closest to Quasimodo have other plans for the gypsy.

Tom Sawyer

Tom Sawyer is the cleverest of characters, constantly outwitting those around him. Then there is Huckleberry Finn, the envy of the town's schoolchildren because he has the rare gift of complete freedom, never attending school or answering to anyone but himself. After Tom and Huck witness a murder, they find themselves on a series of adventures that leads them to some seriously frightening situations.

INTERNET SITES

Do you want to know more about subjects related to this book? Or are you interested in learning about other topics? Then check out FactHound, a fun, easy way to find Internet sites.

Our investigative staff has already sniffed out great sites for you!

Here's how to use FactHound:

1. Visit *www.facthound.com*

2. Select your grade level.

3. To learn more about subjects related to this book, type in the book's ISBN number: **1598890506.**

4. Click the **Fetch It** button.

FactHound will fetch the best Internet sites for you!